The Complete and Utter Truth About the World
and Everything In It

Ian Coulls

The Complete and Utter Truth About the World and Everything In It

Acknowledgements

I would like to express my gratitude to Stephen Matthews of Ginninderra Press, Sharon Kernot, Kate Ryan, Jude Aquilina, David Chapple, Ray Clift, Amy Yang, Christina Barrie, Lorna Lower, Shirley Jansen, Gareth Saunders, Jenny Liu, Kerryn Goldsworthy, Anna Solding, Geoff Goodfellow, Anthony Priwer, Karen O'Neill, Nigel Dey, Martin Christmas, John Malone, Geoff Hastwell, Ken Vincent, North Eastern Writers Inc, Kensington and Norwood Writers Group, Friendly Street Poets and South Australian Writers Centre for their editing, help, advice, support and encouragement.

The Complete and Utter Truth About the World and Everything In It
ISBN 978 1 760417 046 9
Copyright © text Ian Coulls 2015
Ian Coulls can be contacted at manager@holdenhillmedia.com.au

First published 2015 by
GINNINDERRA PRESS
PO Box 3461 Port Adelaide 5015
www.ginninderrapress.com.au

Contents

Hocus Pocus Smocus Jocus

'Here, just a second, Mr Miller. Let me wipe your face.' The nurse took a tissue from the box on the table and wiped away the trail of dribble that festooned ponderously from his chin. A second wipe was necessary when she realised that it had originated from his nose and not his mouth. She slipped the soggy tissue into the plastic bag hanging at the back of his wheelchair.

'Would you like a drink, dear? Here, have some lemon juice.' Nurse Haddon held the spill-proof plastic container while Mr Miller sipped from it. Another wipe was necessary for the new but less snotty dribble that followed. She then noticed that the blanket had slipped from his knees, revealing his drooping lack of modesty. The nurse pulled up the blanket and automatically brushed away his hand as it attempted to snake up her dress.

She released the brake on his wheelchair, moved it to the other side of the garden table and re-applied the brake.

'We'll just move you out of the sun, Mr Miller.'

'I like the sun,' the old man said.

'Yes, well, you'll like this then, dear,' she replied cheerfully and made a tactical retreat to the rear in order to curtail any further discussion.

'Poor Mr Miller,' said one of the other nurses when Nurse Haddon walked back into the ward, 'He's not with it today.'

'I'm not so sure about that,' Louise Haddon said. 'He may not be with us today, but I think he's where he wants to be. He's right with it in his own little world, what's left of it.'

*

Mr Miller sat in the shade unaware that he still had a mouthful of lemon juice. He liked Nurse Haddon. She wore tight uniforms. In earlier years and in moments of semi-lucidity, he might have wondered if it was the uniform that gathered in enthusiastically to embrace her ample breasts, or her ample breasts that yearned to break free and find their way into his hands. All this was now beyond Nathan Miller. He no longer had either the capacity or the energy for this kind of contemplation. He now seemed to spend a lot of time with something in his hand, and wondering what he had intended to do with it.

However, he did like Nurse Haddon. He liked her hair and the way wisps of it refused to be tied back militarily as required. She gave him the time of day, whatever that meant. Maybe she wouldn't give him the time of his life, but he was no longer capable of meeting that challenge anyway. She gave him more human respect than the other nurses did. She asked him questions, she asked his opinion, she told him small everyday things about her husband and her children. She made him feel like he mattered to someone.

He finally realised he still had a mouthful of lemon juice and swallowed it.

It was chilly in the shade of the pine tree. He pulled the blanket up and stared out into the brittle, autumn sunshine. Nathan was elsewhere. Today his inner world was a better place to be.

Nathan was at that party. In his mind, they were all there. There was the chocolate mint liqueur, and Sunny had brought Orange Barrel, that stuff on the blotting paper. There was the port. They were still buying it in flagons in those days, and they would sit down with friends on a Friday night, open the flagon, and throw the cap in the fire.

'Oops! Oh well, guess we'll have to drink it all in one sitting.'

Of course you never felt drunk after having a smoke. In his younger days, Nathan was only a moderate smoker. He would have a few cones, or share a few joints for the first hour or so, but that was usually enough to float him through the evening. He didn't keep smoking like some people.

When he was younger, Nathan hadn't really liked it when people would smoke their way into oblivion. To an endless background of Pink Floyd, they would eventually drift away into peaceful slumber in a sea of velvet scatter cushions on the living room floor.

At one or two in the morning, they would get up and shake his hand at the door. 'Hey, man, that was great. We'll have to do that again some time.'

What was great? What had happened? What had anyone done? Did anyone remember? There had always been that discussion about whether they were *still* listening to 'Set the controls for the heart of the sun' or were they listening to it *again*? What had anyone talked about? Had anyone actually connected with anyone else? Well, yes, some people had, because when he and Carol finally got to bed, they often discovered the wet patch left by some free-range copulaters who had availed themselves of the bed.

And in the morning, they would sometimes find the kettle in the fridge. It was worse when they started to use electric kettles because, instead of just turning it on as most people did, every so often someone would fill it with water, put it on the hotplate and turn the hotplate on. Burning plastic was a poor substitute for incense, and Nathan and Carol would always have to scrape off all the charred remains of the jug before using the hotplate again to spot their hash. However, some tokers didn't seem to care too much about the burnt plastic remains. At times, their biro came so close to the hotplate that it was not certain whether they were spotting hash or spotting molten plastic from the biro.

Nevertheless, Nathan had gradually begun consuming more and more substances to fill up the empty spaces in his life.

So which party was he thinking about on that crystalline autumn morning? Uncertain, but it was one of those parties when they were living in that old farmhouse with all the beautiful land around them. The house was on a hilltop that sloped down to a natural three-hundred-and-sixty-degree amphitheatre. There were orchards, pine forests, a dam, and there was no other house in sight. People would often come out and party on the weekend, but during the week there was blissful solitude.

That Saturday afternoon had been eventful. Sunny had come in his beaten-up old Jaguar. It was a strange possession, given his addiction to the Hare Krishna movement. If it had been an old Holden, Ford or Morris Minor, people would not have raised their eyebrows. But a thrashed-out Jaguar? It was like an out-take from *Withnail and I*.

Anyway, Sunny had come with his Hare Hare friend Sebastian, and had brought along some acid to spend a day in the country. All had gone well at first: the burning of incense, the eating of fruit, the sitting in the sunshine and the making of music. Sunny was an excellent guitarist with a velvety voice, so it was always very pleasant to sit around and listen to him playing. His friend accompanied him through all these rituals and responded with appropriate admiration at all times.

Throughout the afternoon, Sebastian had shown more and more appreciation of Sunny's musical, human and spiritual qualities. However, as the afternoon progressed, his worship seemed to veer noticeably towards Sunny's earthly qualities, and it became obvious that Sebastian would have liked to achieve a more earthy manifestation of their spiritual union.

No one at the farm particularly cared what they did or where they did it, but it was clear that Sebastian was having difficulty coming to grips with his unspoken, earthly desires. Nathan, Carol, Sunny and Sebastian were sitting on the floor in the lounge, drinking coffee. Don and Olivia were sitting on the sofa because Olivia was not a sitting-on-the-floor sort of person, and her husband Don felt that she shouldn't be left to sit alone. There were maybe a dozen other people in the hall, in the kitchen or outside.

By this stage, the acid had really kicked in and the dope was somewhere in the equation as well. The stereo was wound up quite loud and 'Dark Side of the Moon' was adding to the intensity.

The tension between Sebastian and Sunny mounted steadily till it became unbearable and badly in need of resolution. It oozed out of the walls and hung in the air like a dark cloud. The conversation became strained. Sebastian was struggling with the tension and giggling nervously.

Nathan, who was never one for subtlety, decided that enough was enough, and felt he could help matters along. 'Sunny, why don't you take Sebastian for a walk out in the pine forest and let him shag you?'

Olivia was visibly appalled.

Carol was not. She was accustomed to Nathan, but she could see this was not one of his finest moments. She tried to lighten the tone. 'Hey, why don't we all take our clothes off and shag each other.'

Olivia was clearly even more appalled, but this was nothing compared to Sebastian's reaction. His nervous giggling transformed into a shrill peal of hysterical laughter. He picked up the sugar bowl that was sitting on the carpet between the cups of coffee and flung it in the air. It came down with a crash on two of the coffee cups and a glass of port, spilling coffee, port and sugar all over the carpet. Olivia was aghast.

'Hey, it's OK,' said Nathan. 'I'll let the dog in.' He went to the door. 'Fuggly! Fuggly! Come on, boy. Look at this.'

The dog immediately summed up the situation and the social importance of his role. With joyful slurping and snuffling, he made short work of the sticky mess on the carpet.

Olivia may have been just as appalled by this, but she showed signs of coping. 'I'll get a cloth and mop it up,' she said.

'Don't worry, Olivia. We only rescued the carpet from the local dump anyway,' Carol chimed in.

Olivia insisted and people let her insist. It was easier. However, she didn't seem to be especially comforted by the information about the dump. It was noticeable that she spent the rest of the afternoon with her shoes off and her feet up on the sofa. Nathan and Carol felt it was better not to tell her that they had also acquired the sofa from the dump.

Early in the evening, Olivia developed a headache and Don took her home. Nathan hadn't seen Don and Olivia leave. He had been in the pantry with Myra, knocking back the chocolate mint liqueur. The chocolate mint liqueur was exquisite, and if anyone had realised it was there, then very soon it wouldn't have been. Carol wasn't really into it – she was a spirits drinker – so Nathan and Myra stashed the chocolate mint liqueur in the pantry and made numerous visits during the evening to see that it was properly appreciated. Carol had probably seen Don and Olivia off. No one was very sure when Sunny and Sebastian left, but it probably wasn't long after the big spill.

Gradually, most of the visitors drifted away and, at some stage in the early morning hours, Nathan stepped outside to void his bladder in the garden. It was a warm summer evening with a jet-black sky. The stars were slowly turning in the heavens and, as he stood there holding what was his, he gradually came to the realisation that the stars should not have been turning. Well, at least not noticeably turning. However, they were gradually turning faster.

By this time, Nathan realised that it hadn't been a good idea to look up. He had the presence of mind to step aside from the damp patch he had just created in the grass and gradually sank to his knees. It was not a collapse, not even a stumble. It was a deliberate decision to change his perspective on the world. The night sky had been glorious. It had filled him with a tremendous sense of spiritual awe, but had been a little overwhelming. At this moment, it was possibly time to move on from the spiritual to the sensual.

Nathan lay there in the sweet, earthy smell of soil, flowers and summer grass. He was not entirely comfortable, but right then, there wasn't much he could do about it. The Hand of God was upon him, pressing him firmly to the earth so he could fully appreciate the Glory of Nature. In this context, God, His Hand, Nature and its Glory all required the respect of capital letters. Even the smell of stale cat piss had its place in the world, although it was not in quite the same need of capital letters.

For a while he just lay there, the grass prickling his cheek and tickling his nose. Despite the feeling of lockjaw and that acid taste in his mouth, Nathan was at Peace and at One with the World. At this moment, his whole Existence was enhanced by Well Deserved, Appropriate Capital Letters. Now, however, the ground beneath him also started to turn and this aroused a minor hesitation in his moment of spiritual and sensual abandon. His capital letters promptly disappeared. Was he going to throw up? No, he was sure he wasn't going to throw up.

Nathan awoke some time later with a damp cheek. Surely it was nearly morning. There seemed to be a morning dew. He lay there contemplating nature, which now seemed a little less awe-inspiring, dare he say even a little less comfortable. He lay there a moment longer, not so much due to the bliss of his Oneness with the Universe and Everything in It, but more out of uncertainty about his capabilities. And there was still the uncertainty about whether he might externalise the contents of his stomach.

There were now heavy storm clouds, but the moon came out briefly and with it came the gradual understanding that he had already thrown up and was lying in it. It was especially at times like this that one regretted having long hair. He stood up and with his fingers tried to comb his hair. Unfortunately, his hand now contained damp solid matter. He was comforted that it didn't smell like dog shit. This left him with the only slightly preferable understanding that it was his own vomit.

Nature can have its less glorious moments. At this point, Nathan felt that neither nature nor the universe deserved a capital letter. He decided that his last chance for spiritual and sensual unity with the universe would be a long, hot shower. He was tired and his head was throbbing. Regardless of where Carol was, and regardless of anyone else's wet patch, he just wanted to crawl into bed and go to sleep.

Confident that Carol would already be in bed, he knew she would be displeased if he came to bed with his hair full of vomit. A shower was definitely in order. Uncertain as to who might still be present and conscious, he bypassed the lounge. He was not anxious to be seen with his long, flowing locks thus decorated. In the shower, he remembered Carol had gone to bed early, so hopefully there had been no previous squatters and he wouldn't have to avoid the wet patch.

Not really rejuvenated, but slightly less annihilated, Nathan emerged from the shower and walked into the lounge. The room was unoccupied except for Carlotta, a mid-afternoon arrival whom nobody seemed to know, but who had blended seamlessly with festivities and caused no grief. Sleeping on her back on cushions on the floor, she was stoned and drunk, mouth open, snoring slightly, arms spreadeagled and legs going most of the way up to what, he remembered from earlier in the evening, was a very tidy little arse. Nathan was fairly sure that the legs went all the way, but he was unable to know for sure because of the skimpy dress she was wearing. He sank to his knees on the cushions beside her. She stopped snoring.

He sank further on to the cushions and, reclining on one elbow, asked, 'Are you OK? Would you like a blanket?'

'Nnnngh…'

Nathan pulled a blanket off the sofa, revealing a number of cigarette burns and threadbare patches. He returned to the cushions to discover Carlotta had raised her knees. It was true: her legs did go all the way up to her arse. Her knees like her arms were spreadeagled and if she had been blonde, he might not have noticed the wisps of pubic hair that escaped from the haven or maybe the heaven of her briefs. Hesitantly, he covered her modesty, or in this case her immodesty, with the blanket, but compromised by including himself under the blanket. She awoke with a small snort.

'Ngurgh, *danke schön*,' she mumbled and rolled over, throwing her right arm around his waist and bemoaning her inebriated condition. '*Vielleicht habe ich ein bisschen zu viel getrunken.*'

Nathan was not exactly sure what this might mean, but in the best of all worlds it was an invitation to fondle her firm, little buttocks. If on the other hand, so to speak, this was not so, it could lead to an unfortunate social indiscretion. Quandering thusly, he sank back into the cushions and quandered further for some moments. With eyes closed, Carlotta moved still closer and might well have sunk into deeper sleep. Nathan thought that the only decent thing to do was to slip his arm under her head to give her a better pillow.

Carlotta half opened her eyes and nestled closer. She was still very vague and seemed uncertain whether sleep was the first thing on her mind. Nathan wrapped his arms around her and she was awake, but maybe still on another planet. He also was on another planet, but not the same one as Carlotta. There was probably no consent. She was not really aware what the question was. In fact, there had probably not been a question.

There was some fumbling related to clothing. He didn't look into her eyes. Her eyes had seemed vacant. He didn't kiss her. He knew his breath still smelt of vomit. He briefly kissed her earlobe and buried his head in the cushion. Lips and ears and eyes were not in Nathan's lovemaking vocabulary. He probably didn't have any lovemaking vocabulary. Anyway, most of the action took place considerably south of the shoulders. The machinery started to turn.

Carlotta's world also turned, slowly and slightly nauseously. In a romantic novel, they would have looked into each other's eyes and seen a shared world that only they knew. In a romantic novel, it would have been a mixture of love and passion. It would not have been with some spaced-out deadbeat she hardly knew. It seemed to go on forever, but then it all happened at once. He thought he was going to come, and she thought she was going to vomit.

'Stop! Stop! I'm going to be sick.'

Nathan might have continued, but having already been decorated with vomit that evening, he stopped. He withdrew and rolled to one side, but was unable to prevent himself from coming on the blanket.

Carlotta, maybe in some gallant attempt not to throw up on the cushions, rolled in the same direction and threw up all over his shirt. 'Sorry,' she said, streamers of snot trailing from her nose. 'Do you have a handkerchief?'

'Here, use this,' he said, taking off his shirt and offering it to her.

'But it is full of sick.'

'Hey, it's your puke, sweetie,' he replied gallantly.

She used the blanket to wipe her nose. She then blew her nose into it.

'Hey, don't do that!'

'Is OK,' she said. 'Is not my blanket.'

'No, it's… Yeah…never mind…'

Nathan picked up his shirt and the blanket and went out to the laundry. He threw them in the empty washing machine and headed off to the bathroom. Carlotta had beaten him to it and was showering. He presumed it would be OK to share the shower with her. After all, they had just shared the same vagina.

'Fuck off!' came an angry voice from the shower.

'Hey, we just made love…'

'You call that love, you bastard?'

It was true that Carol had sometimes referred to Nathan as a Neanderthal and it was also true that he didn't really have much understanding of how women think, but this was only because he didn't care. He had thought Carlotta wanted it. If she hadn't been into it, how come she had gone ahead? Hadn't they been in Acid Heaven? Had this been Hamburger Love and not the Lamb of God? Such was the poetry jingle-jangling through his poor, aching head.

Nathan went to the bedroom to get another shirt. He quietly opened the door and didn't turn on the light. Even totally spaced out, he could find his way around their own bedroom, and he didn't want to disturb Carol.

He quietly opened the wardrobe and took out a clean shirt. He would wait till after his shower before he put it on, and he would wait in the bedroom for Carlotta to finish before he went back to the bathroom. Then he realised through the spacey haze that he wouldn't need a clean shirt till the morning. He could just put on his pyjama top, which was under his pillow. He put the clean shirt back in the wardrobe, sat on the bed, and reached towards the pillow.

'Ooh, Jesus, get off!'

Nathan had sat on someone and his hand had brushed past a face that had stubble on it. It clearly wasn't Carol.

'Who the hell are you?'

'Fuck off, buddy,' came the reply in a thick American accent.

'Who are you?'

'Fuck off, buddy,'

'This is my bedroom. Who the fuck are you?'

'How'd you like I rearrange your face?'

Nathan went back to the door and turned the light on. Carol was the one without the stubble.

'Who the fuck are you?'

'Are you some kind of stupid? Turn off the light, buddy, and piss off!'

'That's my wife there!'

'Congratulations. Many happy weddings. Many happy wives. Beat it. She's busy.'

'Carol, what's happening here?'

'Hey, buddy, you smell of puke!' his uninvited guest offered uninvitedly.

'Carol, what are you doing?'

'Have a guess, Nathan,' came Carol's reply.

'Carol!'

'Piss off, Nathan.' Carol seemed to be in agreement with her American friend.

Nathan briefly contemplated making some heroic gesture in relation to the intruder, but was not confident of his chances. There didn't seem to be much point in making a heroic gesture if Carol wasn't inclined to ride off with him into the sunset.

'Fuck you both, you lousy bastards!' he said heroically from the door, slamming it closed behind him.

On the radio in the lounge, Chuck Berry was singing 'No particular place to go'. With no particular sense of irony, Nathan stumbled through the lounge and back into the kitchen, where he found Carlotta standing in the middle of the room, staring vacantly at the electric kettle.

'Not in the fridge!' he said helpfully. Then he remembered that he was on the way for his second shower in less than an hour. 'Shower...' he mumbled to no one in particular, and shuffled off into another room of his own bad dream.

In the shower, Nathan's mind churned laboriously through the day's events. *What's she so upset about? She was up for it. She came on to me.*

She'd have been upset if I turned her away, he thought. He stopped short of suggesting she had taken advantage of him while he was under the influence of drugs. Who the hell is she anyway? Never seen her before. Must be a friend of Carol's. It was only then that he showed any sign of indignation that this woman might be an uninvited guest.

*

Carlotta, though not mentally in the same room as the kettle and the fridge, was not entirely confused. By this stage, she was wrestling with guilt, remorse and other manifestations of a strict Lutheran background. She didn't feel she was entirely to blame, but her upbringing left her struggling with a lot of 'should haves' and 'shouldn't haves'. She was angry that all of these behavioural imperatives were directed at her and none at Nathan, who didn't seem to burden himself with any of these issues at all. She definitely hadn't enjoyed it. She shouldn't have let him. Had she let him? She shouldn't have had that smoke, probably shouldn't have had so many drinks. But then she'd had a few smokes before she arrived.

Mein Gott! It was only when she thought about her condition when she arrived that afternoon that she remembered leaving Trudi in the car. It would have been unforgivable if Trudi was a dog, but Trudi was her baby daughter.

The back door splintered against the wall as she burst through it and raced through the pitch-black garden, tripping over a variety of vegetables and other plants, hacking her shins on what might have been the front of a wheelbarrow. There was a gate to the garden enclosure, and she fumbled to find the latch. Three cars were parked in disarray outside the gate but, with the moon behind the clouds, it was hard to tell which was which. She groped desperately at the first one and, finding the door handle, threw the door open. It was not her car.

By the dim inside light of this car, she could see her own car some six or seven metres away. She raced to it. It was locked. Her keys. They weren't in her pocket. She didn't bother wondering where they were. Now fuelled purely by adrenalin, she sank to her knees and groped about in the darkness till she found a reasonable size rock, big enough to fill her hand. She smashed it as hard as she could against the rear side window. There was a crunching sound as the window crazy-cracked, but didn't break.

'*Scheiße! diese modernen Autos!*' She swung again, but the rock, apparently sandstone, crumbled in her hand, breaking a couple of her fingernails.

She groped around desperately and found another rock. Three, four blows and the window finally surrendered. She reached inside and opened the door. Inside there was a bundle of woollen clothing and a shawl. She picked it up and held it to her to give it warmth. She peeled back the shawl to reveal in the faint light of the other car the tiny face of her innocent child. Weeping, she hugged the child and kissed the face, bathing it in warm, salty tears, but to no avail. The face was cold. The body was cold. The child was dead.

Bereft, distraught, hysterical, she raced back into the house, bursting into the bathroom with a clatter. 'Help me! Come quickly!'

There was nowhere to come, nowhere to go. The entire story was there in her arms as she stood in the doorway.

'Jesus Christ!' Nathan was instantly sober. 'Whose baby?'

'It is my baby. She is dead!' sobbed Carlotta.

'Where's it been?'

'In the car. I forget about her and leave her in the car.'

'Bloody hell, are you sure she's dead?'

'*Sie ist tot*, she is dead. I forget about her.'

'What's going on?' came a voice from the doorway. Carol had heard Carlotta's hysterical cries and had come to see what was happening.

'What's up?' came an American voice behind Carol.

'*Sie ist tot!*' wailed Carlotta.

'Shoot! Are you sure?' asked the nameless American, pushing past Carol, and trying to take the inert bundle from Carlotta's arms.

'She is dead. It is my fault!'

'What happened? How did she die?' asked Carol.

'I forget about her. I leave her in the car.'

'Shoot, how could you do that?'

'Give her a break, Linus!' said Carol and turned to Carlotta. 'What are you going to do?'

'What are *we* going to do?' corrected Linus. 'We're all out of our brain and the place is lousy with drugs. Let's get out of here.'

'Let's you get out of here if you like,' snapped Nathan. 'I live here. What are we going to do?'

'We've got to contact the police,' said Carol.

'Don't be stupid. They'll come and find the dope and we'll all be arrested.' Linus was proving to be not entirely heroic.

'Well, we've got to take her to the hospital,' persisted Carol.

'What's the point? She's dead,' Linus argued.

Nathan supported him. 'We can't go to the hospital. They'll call the police.'

The self-interest of the two men exasperated Carlotta. 'I'm going to take her to the hospital,' she sobbed.

'You can't do that,' argued Nathan. 'You'll get us all arrested.'

'*Fick dich!* What would you do, you bastard? Throw her in the rubbish bin? *Du bist ein verdammter Arschloch!* Carlotta knew she was in trouble, and was shaping up to take Nathan with her. 'You rape me.'

'He what?' Carol blurted out.

'He rape me, the bastard! I tell the police everything.' Carlotta was now going to share her unhappiness with as many people as possible.

'Hey, I'm out of here,' said Linus.

*

'…Mr Miller, Mr Miller,' someone said in a singsong voice. 'Here's your medicine.' It was Nurse Haddon. 'Mr Miller, you're sweating. Oh dear, you're all sweaty. We'd better get you inside. You're going to catch a cold out here.'

'Carlotta! Carlotta, I'm sorry! It wasn't me. I didn't do it.'

'I'm not Carlotta, Mr Miller. I'm Nurse Haddon. What didn't you do, love?' the nurse replied.

'I didn't do it. It was Linus. Please forgive me.'

'Who's Linus, Mr Miller? Here, calm down. You're all upset.'

'Please forgive me. I'm sorry!'

'If you didn't do it, you needn't be sorry, dear. There's nothing to forgive.'

'But I didn't rape Carlotta. She came on to me. I didn't want to. That's why she killed herself. It was nothing to do with the baby.'

'What baby, Mr Miller?'

'My wife didn't believe me about Carlotta, but Carol was always going to go off with Linus anyway.'

'Come on, love, you're getting all worked up and not making much sense. Here, let's take you inside.'

Nurse Haddon released the brake on the wheelchair and noticed that the blanket had once again slipped off his knees. She was coming around to put it back in place when Nathan launched himself sideways at her. He threw his arms around her waist and, startled, she leapt back, dragging him with her and overturning the wheelchair. He clung to her, but not dangerously. He was on his knees with his arms around her waist, desperately imploring her.

'I'm sorry, I'm sorry! I didn't mean to… It was Linus. That's why she killed herself. I promise I won't say about the baby… It wasn't me.'

The other nurses and an attendant came racing from the nurses' station and restrained him, his contorted face bathed in tears and snot. Nurse Haddon struggled free. It was becoming harder to sympathise. This was not the first time he had lost the plot. There had been a long history of it.

'He's such a waste of oxygen,' said one of the other nurses.

'Oh, I don't know,' said Carol Haddon. 'Look at all the jobs and income he's generated for police and lawyers and doctors and pathologists and nurses.'

'Yeah, but the police and nurses get paid bugger all and the nurses are the only ones who actually give a stuff about these poor, stupid bastards.'

Carol Haddon sighed. 'That's life.'

The Smell of Soap

Mr Reid was a librarian. He lived across the road from us when I was a child. I knew he lived across the road, but I never saw him there. He was a widower and he was always at work. As there was no Mrs Reid, it was an empty house. It was Mr Reid's house.

I saw Mr Reid when I went to the library with my mother. He was an old English gentleman, very gentle. He always wore a suit and tie, as was the custom with respectable people in those days. Respectable people wore suits and took their hat off when they went indoors. They raised their hat when they greeted a lady. Librarians were respectable people and so he would have had to wear a suit, but in my childlike innocence I was sure he was respectable anyway, suit or no suit.

While my mother looked for books, he would often take me on his lap and read to me. He had a soft, powdery voice, smelt of soap, and he always knew which books would be interesting. It is possible that they weren't always interesting, but they were interesting when he read them. While he was reading, I would play with the buttons on his coat and, eventually, lean back on his shoulder to hear the story he was reading. He would ask me questions about the story and the people in it. It was not a test. He just asked my opinion about things. What did I think would happen? What would I do in this situation? If there were pictures in the books, he would ask me about them. Who did I think this was? What did I think they were doing? I loved his books and his stories. They were our stories.

It is hard to know when Mr Reid's story began, because we only went to the library when my mother had finished reading her current books. Whether this was measured in weeks or months was meaningless to a child, for whom time was an irrelevance, an indefinable continuum that had little other effect than the causation of boredom.

The fact that he was not at the library must have been something of a disappointment on some particular occasion, as it would have been on following occasions. The memory of these things for a child can be quite short, and so subsequent absence would have gone unnoticed. Children adapt quickly to the changing world around them.

At some stage, however, I must have wondered where Mr Reid was. On reflection, I realise that it may have been years before this occurred to me. I asked a neighbour, but she told me to ask my father. I don't remember asking my father, but it was he who told me. I'm sure my mother was dead by then.

I understand why they wouldn't have told me at the time. These things weren't discussed then. Mr Reid had been arrested and put on trial for interfering with children. Before this, no one had ever explained what interfering with children was. I didn't have time to feel any revulsion concerning Mr Reid because, by the time my father told me, he was able to tell me the full story.

Of course, my father never told me the lurid detail of what Mr Reid was supposed to have done or how often. However, the fact was, Mr Reid was found to be innocent. The allegations had been malicious. This was not a victory for the old man, who went home, crippled with unspeakable embarrassment, and hanged himself. I had been taken inside and had not seen the ambulance come and go.

With the innocence of a child, I accepted this and moved on. I had loved his stories. I was glad that he had been proved innocent and sad that he was gone. It seemed very unfair, but as a child my understanding was so limited.

Later, I imagined what it must have been like to return alone to an empty house. He would not have been able to go back to his job and serve a community that had turned on him so vehemently. It would have been mortifying for him to go to the local shop to buy groceries. As an older man, it would not have been easy to go somewhere else and start again. He would have sat at home alone and wept.

My father never talked about it again, and I never asked him. We were not a family that talked about these things. We were not a family that talked about anything at all. We were not a family. I don't know what the local community thought about an old man, falsely accused, who had felt so alone and maligned that he had taken his own life. This was not something that a young boy could ask, and certainly not a question they would answer. However, I still remember his lovely stories, his soft voice, and the smell of soap.

Martindale Man

I loved Joanne. She was not a classic beauty, but she had something that drew me to her. She was blonde with a very pale – almost anaemic – complexion, but there was something in her enigmatic smile that, despite her warm, gentle nature, hinted the electricity that lay within. When she made love, she gave herself completely and floated, taking you with her out into the void. When you thought you had nothing left, she would take you again, drawing sensation that seemed to come from your toes and beyond.

Joanne gave herself to me a number of times, but only on loan. I think they were times of her own personal need, but I would have been there for her regardless, any time, any place. She had her own demons, but there was one demon in particular. She was attracted to a handsome law student who knew it: knew he was attractive and knew she was attracted. She was perhaps not the most beautiful song in his playlist, but he let her come to him when it was convenient or when he was at a loose end.

This on-again off-again relationship as one of the Marcus Barrington 'string of polo ponies' tore Joanne apart, but she knew she was not high on his list of conquests. Many women liked him and he liked being liked. He took advantage of all these women with little thought of forming a longer-lasting relationship with any of them. Under the circumstances, Joanne allowed herself a few other friends as consolation. I say 'a few' other relationships, because it was the early seventies, because I thought her beautiful and because, to me, it was inconceivable that no other men would be attracted. I felt she could choose any man she liked, and I didn't dare flatter myself that, apart from her impossible flame Marcus, I was the only man she allowed to come to her.

It is now more than forty years since she last shared her bed with me, but I still remember one special night as if it were yesterday. I had just been posted as a teacher in the country town of Burra. During the long summer holidays, while I was looking for a more permanent dwelling, I was living in Martindale Hall near Mintaro, some thirty kilometres from Burra.

On that night, I had driven a hundred and thirty kilometres from Martindale Hall to Adelaide in order to see a Jethro Tull concert. Rather than drive all the way back that night, I rather disgracefully presented myself unannounced at Joanne's door in the hope I could stay overnight. Her care and generosity exceeded my hopes. I spent the night in her bed and her embrace.

To read these things now, it sounds like all was taken and nothing given, but I had not gone with lust in mind and, in fact, it was Joanne who was in need. It seems selfish to have been so happy to comfort her, but she wept in my arms well into the night, unburdening herself of her anguish. She was such a soft, gentle woman. It was wrenching to hear her unwrap her feelings, to feel her sobbing body racked with torment. Finally, she fell asleep in my arms. But in the half-light of morning she came to me, maybe as a friend, maybe just seeking the solace she had hoped from Marcus, maybe even imagining me as Marcus. I asked no questions.

*

Martindale Hall, where I had been living, was a pseudo-Georgian manor, dignified but not grand. It had been bequeathed to the University of Adelaide, but needed a lot of work. I had been living there as part of a work party, being paid nothing but paying nothing for accommodation. We painted fences and railings, dug trenches for new plumbing, did odd jobs. Marcus Barrington was also a member of this work party.

Regardless of the work, it was an easy-going life. We would come down the grand central staircase in the morning and have breakfast at a long mahogany table lit by a magnificent chandelier. There were rust stains on some of the lower lustres of the chandelier and we liked to imagine that these were not rust stains, but the remains of a projectile vomit. In the evenings we would sometimes retire to the smoking room or the drawing room and read or listen to music. Some evenings we would play snooker in the billiard room. Most evenings there was eating and drinking and smoking.

Meanwhile, however, in Adelaide, not everyone approved of this lifestyle. Some of the Martindale work party were or had been law students, and their left-wing friends disapproved of the way their comrades had sold out and adopted this dissolute, aristocratic lifestyle. The work party had clearly abandoned their socialist principles and become 'lords of the manor'.

By this time, I had discovered and moved out to a small farmhouse some thirty kilometres away, and was driving daily to my workplace in Burra. However, due to the long university holidays, the work party continued their occupation of Martindale Hall. Late in these holidays, I was invited to a back to uni party at the hall. I don't think it was regarded as a particularly special occasion. Parties at the hall were a weekly, sometimes nightly occurrence, just another excuse to drink and smoke. Unknown to the residents, word of this soirée had reached Adelaide, and a 'rescue expedition' had been organised to drive to Martindale Hall, remonstrate with these recalcitrant students and convince them of the folly of their aristocratic ways.

On the day of the celebration, I was already at the hall when they arrived. Most of the inhabitants had already spent the afternoon practising their drinking and smoking and were inside preparing food. I was at the front door with a chicken leg in one hand and a flagon of Four Crown port in the other. As the two cars pulled up, I descended the stairs with as much dignity as one could when holding a half-eaten leg of chicken and a flagon of port.

Since I was no longer living at the hall, I was not considered to be one of the recalcitrants and was warmly greeted by a tall, bespectacled law student.

'G'day, Uncle. How ya going? Where is everyone?'

'Inside cooking up something to eat. Come in. They'll be really pleased to see you.' At this stage I knew nothing of their intention to liberate us or to liberate Martindale Hall.

'So what's happening here?' the inquisition began. 'We heard people here were all forgetting themselves and pooncing about like aristocracy.'

'Sounds like a lotta bullshit, Len. Come in and we'll get some glasses. I need help to drink this.'

'We don't need any of that pompous shit. We brought our own paper cups.'

'Don't waste them. We've got Vegemite glasses. Hope you weren't expecting crystal.'

I don't clearly remember how many people filed past me. I don't remember all that much about the evening, but I remember Joanne's warm smile as she came up the steps. The others continued into the hall, but she stopped and kissed me gently on the cheek.

'How are you?' she asked.

'Zonked,' I replied poetically.

We went inside and got lost in the festivities. The moral and political discussions had not lasted very long and had segued seamlessly into a rambling celebration of life in general and nothing in particular. The rescue party had brought their own food, booze, smokes and music to mark the liberation of the hall.

I had lost contact with Joanne for what might have been a couple of hours when I walked into the entrance hall. She was coming down the grand central staircase. We would have clinked our champagne flutes in salutation, but I was drinking from a Vegemite glass, Joanne from a cardboard cup and we were both drinking cheap port.

Together we walked into the billiard room. Marcus was with an attractive red-haired woman. She was leaning back against the billiard table with her feet apart and her dress around her hips. She seemed to be looking up in wonder at something on the ceiling. Marcus's feet were between hers and he was stooping slightly at the knees. We could see his trousers seemed to be lower than usual and his shirt tail was hanging out.

Hearing us enter, Marcus looked over his shoulder. He winked, and I wasn't sure whether it was directed at Joanne or me. 'Would you guys mind excusing us for a while? We're busy.'

The woman glared at Joanne, made a number of sensuous, pumping movements with her hips and held Marcus closer. She was making it very clear that Marcus was her property and trespassers were not welcome.

I turned to Joanne and her distress was obvious. In her situation, I would have been mortified, and I sensed that Marcus was wallowing in the jealousy generated by this encounter. Joanne's expression crumpled, her cheeks flushed and tears welled in her eyes.

I took her hand and led her into the kitchen. 'I think I need help. I've had too much to drink,' I said. 'Let's make some coffee and go up on the roof. It's beautiful up there on a clear night.'

Joanne wasn't fooled by my fake appeal for help, but we bumbled around in the kitchen and made two beakers of very bad instant coffee.

I took her hand again. 'Come with me. You have to see this.'

I led her through the much less lavish servants' quarters and up a service staircase that led to the roof. It was a warm, clear night and above the roof was a black canopy, spangled with pincushion stars. I closed the door and the high-volume Led Zeplin album that was filling every corner of every room inside the hall disappeared and was replaced by the chirping of the crickets and the occasional mating calls of the peacocks down in the garden.

'Are you OK?'

'Well, yes and no. I'm pretty much over Marcus. For one thing, it's fairly obvious that it's not going to happen for me. For another thing, he's really been such a complete bastard, and not just towards me. But most of all, there's another man and he's really nice.'

'Hey, great.' I was happy for her and disappointed for me. 'How long has this been happening?'

'Oh, I've known him for a couple of years, but it just got serious in the last couple of months. I really like him.'

'But I can tell you're not happy right now.'

'Well, it wasn't just that woman's gloating display of ownership. It was… I could tell she knew who I was. She knew how I felt about Marcus and she was mocking me. I felt like I'd been stripped bare. He's talked about me, and maybe it was true and maybe it wasn't, but fuck him.'

I already knew that Marcus talked about his conquests. Joanne was wound really tight. I took her in my arms and held her close.

'Don't look at me,' she said. 'My eyes are all red and puffy.'

'Doesn't matter. You're still beautiful and I'm sure this new guy thinks so. Everyone loves you, Joanne. Forget about Marcus. He's a turd.'

I sat her down and pointed up at the clear summer sky. 'Hey, look at this. Look at these stars. They're all yours. It's a beautiful world and it's going to be here for the rest of your life. Especially with this new guy who's just walked into it.'

Everything inside me wanted that man to be me, but I knew it wasn't and that had to be all right. At that moment she needed me, but just as a friend.

Then what seemed like two spotlights scanned the sky. This was not Nature. I stood up and went to the parapet. Joanne joined me. There was a car approaching slowly along the drive. At first we just saw the headlights and not the car behind it. Then as the car drew up to the hall, Joanne recognised the car.

'It's Barry,' she said and raced downstairs.

From the roof I saw her emerge from the building and throw her arms around a man. They kissed for longer than I wanted to watch and then disappeared into the building.

With mixed feelings, I made my way back to the party. All ideas of revolution and rescue expedition had now been completely forgotten amidst the party haze. A number of the bedrooms were occupied. There were half a dozen people trying to share a bathtub at the same time. Some had retained the modesty of their underwear or part of it. Some had dispensed with all pretence.

The Adelaide rescue squad had shown the foresight to bring several takeaway pizzas and I remembered seeing some leftovers in the kitchen. I decided I needed pizza. In the kitchen doorway, somebody had managed a spectacular spew that had splattered up the wall. Still in public service mode, I thought I ought to clean it up. I had been immunised against nausea by the cocktail of substances I had previously ingested. Too late it occurred to me that it had not been a good idea to mop up red wine vomit and pieces of half-digested kabana with a tea towel. I astutely reasoned that I could not be reproached for this if no one found the tea towel. I wrapped it in a couple of sheets of newspaper and threw it in the outside rubbish bin.

I came back inside and walked into the drawing room. Joanne was smiling and tears were streaming down her cheeks. I didn't know what Barry had said to her, but it had clearly made her happy.

'Sean, come in and meet Barry. Barry, this is Sean. He's a good friend of mine.'

It seemed that Barry had made Joanne an offer that she didn't even need to think about. The offer was active from right then. The plan was that she would collect her things, they would get into his car and they would drive away into a blissful future that would last the rest of their lives.

After we had consumed more bad coffee, I walked out the front door to wish them well and see them off. As the tail lights disappeared slowly down the long drive, I saw Marcus watching from an upstairs bedroom window. I would like to think he was disappointed or even slightly jealous, but I suspect it was more his injured pride.

The Engagement Present

Ryan arrived unexpected at the Williamstown farmhouse late in the afternoon. He brought some Purple Dots, a strain of acid that had been going around recently. He didn't bring his girlfriend Helen. He said she was busy.

Well, never mind, Evan and Sky thought. They should do justice to this acid and then maybe have a meal. Ryan suggested they listen to the Joni Mitchell *Blue* album and they smoked a few cones to help pass the time until the Purple Dots kicked in.

Eventually, Evan decided it would be a good idea to heat up the stew, which he had already prepared before Ryan's arrival. They often prepared enough for two nights, so there would easily be enough for Ryan.

With Joni Mitchell at high volume, Evan went into the kitchen and muddled the rest of the meal together. There was an old wood stove, so it took some time to light a fire and get the stew going. He thought they might have another cone or two while they were waiting for the stew, and felt coffee would go well with the dope. By this time, his concentration was shot, so the coffee took a little longer than might be expected.

Having finally succeeded in making the coffee, Evan realised that the Joni Mitchell had finished. He put the three mugs of coffee on a tray and went into the lounge. No one was there. Puzzled, he put the tray on the coffee table and looked out the window. Maybe they had walked past him in the kitchen and gone outside. No one in the garden.

Evan heard shuffling from up the passage and went in its general direction. From the passage, the first door on the left was their bedroom and, lo and behold, the mystery was solved. The shuffling and creaking he had heard from the lounge was perfectly synchronised to the rise and fall of Ryan's heaving buttocks. He was enthusiastically entering Sky's personal space.

Although the acid had slowed down Evan's reaction time, it didn't take him long to realise that he was displeased by this turn of events. He decided almost immediately that Ryan needed to be removed from within Sky. The blissful couple were sideways on the double bed. Ryan had not removed his boots, and his jeans were still around his knees.

Evan grabbed the back of Ryan's jeans and pulled. The jeans came down further, but he had not succeeded in disengaging Ryan from the object of his attention. He took hold of Ryan's feet and pulled him backwards off the bed. During this trajectory, Ryan's face briefly replaced his genitalia in Sky's, before he hit the floor with a thud.

Now it was Ryan who was displeased. He stood up and flicked back his long hair. 'Jesus Christ! What did you do that for?'

'It just seemed like a good idea at the time. You're an arsehole, Ryan.'

'What's the trouble, man? What're you so upset about?'

'What d'ya think, arsehole? Is this what you came for?'

'No, man, I just thought it would be good to come and share some acid.'

'Yeah, right, and help yourself to a share of Sky.'

Sky opened her mouth to speak, but decided not to.

'You just came to plant your pointer, man. Suppose you just pull your pants up and fuck off.'

'Hey, no need to be like that. We were just being friendly.'

'Yeah? With friends like you, who needs enemas?'

'Oh, come on, man!'

'Fuck off, Ryan. Get your stuff and fuck off!'

Ryan got his stuff and fucked off.

Sky said nothing. There really wasn't much to say. She took off the rest of her clothes and climbed under the sheets. She shrugged, looked up at Evan and said, 'Don't suppose you want to finish the job for him?'

'You suppose right, Sky. I'm not into batting on a sticky wicket.'

As they say in those novels, 'It was a dark and stormy night'. Sky rolled over and faced the wall. Neither of them slept well, but nothing was said. In the morning, Sky packed her things and went.

*

It was OK. Evan and Sky's relationship hadn't been going that well lately anyway. As it turned out, Sky went back to her previous boyfriend Wally. Gradually Evan realised he had been used to make Wally jealous.

Evan needed a few days of peace and quiet to calm down, and the farmhouse was perfect for this. He felt, however, that he hadn't finished with Ryan. He would go to the Collinswood house shared by Ryan and his girlfriend Helen and speak his mind to Ryan in front of her.

Helen was a young university student, not long out of high school. She was into literature and Ryan was into theatre. She played guitar well and sang gorgeous versions of Joni Mitchell and Leonard Cohen songs.

*

Number six. Ryan and Helen's street sloped up to North East Road and Evan's handbrake was almost useless, so he parked in gear. At the front door, he took a deep breath and rang the doorbell. From the veranda, he could hear Dylan's 'Blood on the tracks' wafting out from an open window. The door opened and a cheerful face appeared.

'Evan, how are you? Ryan's not home. Come through to the kitchen. I'm writing an assignment.'

'I won't stay long, then. Don't want to interrupt while you're having fun.' This was not in the plan. He needed time to think. 'I wouldn't mind a cup of coffee, though.'

They went into the kitchen and Helen bustled around stacking books, folders, papers and a writing pad into one corner of the table. Evan was going to comment on the wisdom of listening to music while studying or writing assignments, but thought better of it.

Having bustled around with the books, Helen now bustled around with the coffee. Lots of nervous energy. 'How's Sky?'

'We split.'

'Oh hell, that's terrible. How come? How long were you together?'

'About a year, but hey…' Evan had planned a dramatic exposition of that week's events, in which, with Helen as a horrified spectator, he once again told Ryan what he thought of him and why. Without Ryan, though, there didn't seem to be much point proceeding. Ryan was his target, not Helen.

'Yeah well, these things happen,' he mumbled. He cursed himself inwardly. Maybe he'd needed to say something that would still leave it open to come back some other time and have his dramatic moment.

Helen was hesitant, almost apologetic. 'Well, I guess it's not such a good time to tell you our news. Anyway, you probably know already.'

'No, what news?'

She couldn't help herself. A radiant beam spread across her cherubic face. 'Ryan probably told you about it when he was up at your place earlier in the week, but you know he came home early. He said he just couldn't wait to get back and propose to me. We're going to get married!'

Evan sat for a moment with a beaker of coffee halfway to his open mouth. He realised he needed to say something appropriate. 'Hey, that's great. Congratulations, Helen.'

She stood at the end of the table looking disappointed by his response. He got up and enveloped her in a big, warm hug, partly because it was the thing to do, partly because he was genuinely happy for this young, innocent woman, and partly to conceal his own emotional disarray. He sat down again and Helen was still beaming, but tears were glistening in her eyes.

'How strange that you should split, though. Ryan came home and said he had seen how happy you two were together and he just knew he loved me and we should get married.'

A Brother's Help

'Mr Hedley! Mr Hedley!' She was a cheerful, little blonde girl.

Gordon Hedley took a step backward. The girl's energy level seemed to exceed what might be considered appropriate in the classroom. It was his first German lesson with this class and he was just trying to connect names with faces and get a feeling who they might be.

'Yes, what's your name please?'

'I'm Kelly Lane. Mr Hedley, do you know Bruce Lane?'

Uh-oh. Gordon Hedley did remember Bruce Lane. Bruce Lane was one of his former students from the first school he had taught in. The connection was obvious and it was not one that teachers necessarily look forward to. This was likely to be evidence that Gordon was getting older. There was no avoiding the question.

'Hello, Kelly, and how do you know Bruce?'

A radiant beam. 'He's my father.'

Damn. Oh well, there it was. It was always going to happen at some stage. This was the first time Gordon would teach the offspring of one of his former students.

'Ah well, you're a very lucky lady, Kelly. Bruce was a fine, young lad. Say g'day. Please pass on my best wishes.'

Young Kelly glowed with pride. The relationship proved positive. The girl clearly wanted to impress her teacher and didn't want to let her father down. This stimulus was unnecessary, however, as she was an intelligent life form and had her own ambitions in life. Kelly studied well across the years, always achieving a high standard. She had a strong personal interest in German and continued to study it all the way through to Year 12.

During this final year, Mr Hedley organised a German camp in the Adelaide Hills. It was a winter camp, and on the final night they were all drinking coffee or hot chocolate and warming themselves in front of a blazing log fire.

Gordon Hedley had now advanced another five years towards death and was gradually becoming accustomed to reminiscence. He reminded young Kelly of the cruel blow she had dealt him on that first day. He chortled away, now quite at ease revealing to her his discomfort at being reminded of the passing years.

The pause which followed was slightly longer than one might have expected. Hedley looked up and saw Kelly staring wryly into her hot chocolate.

Finally, she finished the chocolate, turned her back to the fire and broke the silence. 'Yes, well, actually, it seems that Bruce isn't my father after all. He's my uncle.'

Love in the Stables

Philippe Lenoir was a good man. Like his father, Henri, he was a stable hand in the retinue of the Marquis de Montreuil on the outskirts of Paris. His mother had died when he was young, so it fell to his father to raise him as best he could. Philippe's finer qualities, his father insisted, were inherited from his mother, who, though only a kitchen hand, had been a wonderful woman. Nevertheless, without the support of his beloved wife Mathilde, Henri had done his best and Philippe loved and respected him.

Philippe was a fine-looking young man. As he approached manhood, it was clear that he would have little difficulty finding a wife. Many of the young women in the Marquis's service found him attractive and, lacking the refinement of those of higher birth, often expressed their interest in ways that would make people of his father's generation blush. Being a normal, high-spirited youth, Philippe would at times take advantage of the frank appreciation of these women.

From childhood, however, Philippe had developed and maintained a friendship with Caroline Labelle, a young woman who had become one of the Marchioness de Montreuil's chambermaids. Although they were now both adult, their relationship had retained its innocence. Caroline was a charming woman, attractive, warm and generous. Philippe's father had always felt she would be a splendid wife for his son.

Most people in the service of the Marquis de Montreuil had very little spare time. However, on occasions when their paths crossed in the course of their household duties, Philippe and Caroline would pause and chat. There was always something to laugh about.

*

There came a time when Philippe noticed a serious change in Caroline's mood. For some weeks she had been strangely distant, almost unapproachable.

'Are you ill, Caroline?' Philippe asked. 'Have you forgotten how to smile?'

'I'm all right, Philippe. I'm well.'

'You're not all right, Caroline. Can't we talk? Are we no longer friends?'

'Philippe, please, there is no problem.' But her lip quivered and tears began to well in her eyes.

'We're friends, Caroline. You can tell me.'

'Not here, Philippe. I can't tell you here.'

'Then come into the stables.'

'No, not into the stables. People will think ill of us.'

'Then tell me here, Caroline. Just smile and no one will know.'

She smiled, but two streams of tears wound their way down her cheeks. 'Philippe, I'm too ashamed. Even you won't want to know me.'

'I'm your friend. I'll always be your friend. You can tell me anything.'

There was a long pause. 'Philippe, I am undone,' she sobbed. 'The Master has destroyed my virtue.'

Philippe was at the same time bereft and furious. His hands were shaking with rage, but he needed to be calm for Caroline. 'Your virtue isn't lost. Virtue is a quality that can't be stolen. A warm, caring heart can still be warm and caring, even if a cold, uncaring person has hurt it. What has happened?'

Caroline's lips quivered and she put her hand to her mouth. Her shoulders were shaking and her chest was heaving.

Philippe smiled warmly and spoke softly. 'There's no hurry. Take your time.'

'The Mistress wanted to go for a walk in the park and the Master said she should take Diane, her personal maid, with her. Then he told me that the carpet in his room had not been cleaned properly. When I went to his room, he took me in his arms and told me he wanted to become my lover. I told him I was not willing and tried to free myself, but he held me firmly and pushed me on to his bed. I was terrified and screamed, but no one seemed to hear. I was helpless and he forced himself on me. I could do nothing. It was horrible. It was so degrading.'

'He's a monster. I'll kill him.'

'No, Philippe, no. It will serve no purpose. It will only cause us all more grief.'

'He's defiled you. He can't be allowed to get away with this.'

'Philippe, he said if I refused him, he'd dismiss my parents and me from the estate and see that I don't find work anywhere in the region.'

'Perhaps it's better to go somewhere else. I'll come with you and we can take your parents.'

'Philippe, my parents are too old and the Master will punish your own father.'

Philippe was furious, but felt that he could do nothing without the agreement of Caroline, and he didn't want to compromise his father's employment in the stables. He became thoughtful and brooding. Although Philippe's relationship with his father was close and loving, he did not tell him all this immediately. He knew it was not Caroline's fault and he did not want his father to think ill of her.

As the weeks passed, however, Caroline became more and more distressed. This did not escape Philippe's attention.

'Caroline, I understand your anger and your pain, but no one needs to know. And anyway, everyone knows what an animal the Master is. You're not the only one. No one will blame you. I'll still be your friend.'

Caroline could no longer repress her anguish. The tears flooded down her cheeks. 'Philippe, I'm with child. It's his. I don't want his disgusting child. I don't want to live.'

'Come with me.' Philippe was not interested what anyone else thought. He took her hand and led her into the stables. Once inside, he found an empty stall, put his arm around her and led her into it. 'Caroline, you mustn't think like this. Listen, we can sort it out. You're not alone.'

She was unable to hold back the tears. 'I am, I am. I feel so alone.'

'You're not alone, Caroline. I love you.' He had thought about this for weeks, but hadn't meant to say it so soon. The words just came out naturally and felt so right.

'Philippe, there's nothing we can do. I feel so miserable.' Either she had not heard his disclosure, or it was something she already knew in her own heart.

Philippe continued. This was not the time to discuss his feelings or their relationship. 'We must speak to our parents. We need permission to leave here. We must go somewhere else.'

'We?'

'We, Caroline. I'll come with you. I'll marry you.'

'But people will mock you. They'll say you have been cuckolded.'

'No, they won't. We'll say the child is ours.'

Caroline's eyes opened wide. She stood in silence. It was only now that she realised the enormity of what Philippe was saying. She gathered herself together. 'My parents will hate me. I've disgraced them. How can I tell my parents? I'm so ashamed.'

'We'll speak to my father first. He'll understand.'

They went to Henri. Philippe explained to him what had happened and told him of his feelings for Caroline. Having worked for the Marquis for so long, his father was not surprised, but was infinitely proud of his son. He told Caroline she must trust her parents. She was such a fine young girl, he knew her parents must love her very much. Henri said they should go quickly to talk with her parents, but that he would first make some soup. They could eat together with her parents as a family. The matter was best resolved before it became obvious that she was with child.

Henri had not known Caroline's parents very well, but he was right. They were, of course, greatly distressed, but they loved their daughter dearly. Her father showed more concern about appearances, but her mother, although upset, clearly understood the situation. They all knew from their years of service that Caroline would have had very little chance of resistance if the Master had lusted after her. Initial explanations concluded, they sat down, shared Henri's soup and the Labelle family's bread and discussed what needed to be done.

It was not just a question of parental consent. Henri readily gave his consent to Philippe marrying Caroline, and her parents quickly saw that this was the only way to preserve everyone's dignity. Caroline had an uncle with whose family they could live for a while, until Philippe found a job and somewhere to live. But the couple would need permission to leave the estate. Clearly, there was little point approaching the Marquis over the issue. He would do everything possible to prevent his prey from escaping. They needed to speak to Her Ladyship. They hoped she would be more sympathetic. Philippe said he would do this, but Henri said it would be more fitting, as his father, that he go and plead on behalf of the couple.

*

'And so you see, Your Ladyship, because the lass is with child, both families would be extremely grateful if the couple were allowed to live with relatives off the estate until they can marry decently and establish themselves.'

The Marchioness knew who Philippe was, but did not look entirely convinced. 'So how pregnant is this girl?'

'Perhaps some six weeks, two months, Milady.'

'And where might this clandestine event have taken place?'

'I don't know, Milady,' Henri replied, tempted, but not daring to add that he was not present at the time.

'Come now, a chambermaid and a stable hand don't have that many opportunities to become intimate.'

'Well, I suppose it must have been in the stables, Milady.'

'Charming! And what, pray tell, apart from being indiscreet with a stable hand, would a chambermaid be doing in the stables? Did no one notice? Did no one find it strange that a chambermaid might be in the stables? How many of our chambermaids are frequenting the stables, may I ask?'

'I don't know, Milady. I just know that the girl is with child by my son and, as his father, I come to beg this kindness of you.'

'And why have you come?'

'I am the boy's father, Milady.'

'Indeed, and have you fathered his child?'

'No, Milady, I just –'

'Just send me the boy. Is he a boy or a man? Can he not speak for himself?'

'He can, Milady. I'll send him.'

The Marchioness was clearly very angry. 'Send him to my chamber.'

*

Philippe, washed and in his Sunday clothes, stood before Her Ladyship. She sat down at a stylish mahogany table. On the table was a beautifully crafted decanter, containing some sort of red wine. Next to the decanter was a stemmed glass from which the Marchioness had already consumed most of the contents. She picked up the decanter and refilled the glass, her hand trembling slightly. Philippe shifted nervously from foot to foot, his eyes downcast.

Finally, she spoke. 'So is this girl with child?'

'Yes, Milady.'

'And is this your doing?'

'Yes, Milady.'

'And were you with her when this happened?'

'Of course, Milady. How could it be otherwise?'

There was a pause. 'And where was His Lordship when this happened?'

There was a longer pause. 'I don't know, Your Ladyship. I don't understand.'

'Yes, you do, Philippe. Where was my husband when this child was fathered?'

'I don't know, Milady. I don't understand.'

'Do you want my help, boy, or don't you?'

'Yes, Milady. I do.'

The Marchioness paused and finished what was left of the wine in her glass. Her gaze lingered on Philippe's handsome countenance and his firm, youthful figure. Her voice had been harsh and brittle, but now her tone softened. 'Do you love this girl, Philippe?'

'I do, Milady.'

'Does she love you?'

'She does, Milady.'

'Do you wish to marry her?'

'I do, Milady.'

'Philippe, you are my servant. I am your Mistress, but in the privacy of this room I will speak to you more frankly than I have ever before spoken to a person of your low rank. You are a lucky man. Caroline is a beautiful young woman, and she loves you. You love her. In this respect, you are more wealthy, more lucky than I am. You have both made this choice to marry. You may not believe it, but this was not a choice that I was allowed. In my world, women are possessions. We are pawns to be bartered and traded for strategic advantage. I am here, I am the Marquis's wife, I am the Mistress of this house because my father gave me to the Marquis.

'I am my husband's connection with a wealthier, more powerful, more prestigious world. But in our own house, I'm just another of his trophies, another of his toys, to be enjoyed when it pleases him, and to be put aside for other toys when he becomes bored. I'm sure you have little sympathy for a lady of my rank, but my life is not as joyful as most people think.

'I've never known the joy of a man who loves me for myself, who loves me for who I am inside. I've never known the joy, the ecstasy that some say is possible in the embrace of a man. Your Caroline is not the first local wench my husband has deflowered and I'm sure she won't be the last. She's already just another of many, all of whom he has abandoned when he wearies of their novelty. And I must stand aside and accept this indignity. On the other hand, it is inconceivable to him that I might find passion in the arms of a lover, a younger man than he, a more robust man than he. Inconceivable and unacceptable.

'However…' she paused, 'accept it he will. Today, Philippe, for just this one time, you will be my lover. You will not tell your Caroline. You will tell no one else. My standing and my reputation must not be sullied. But he will know. And he will accept it. He will not want it known that his wife has taken a younger man, a stable hand, as a lover. Nor will he put me aside, because he will not dare to put my father aside. Without my father's goodwill, he is nothing. And I shall see that you are both safe in the court of my father.'

The Marchioness was older than Philippe, but not yet forty. Younger, she must have been a radiant belle, but much of her youthful beauty still remained. Philippe found it hard to believe that a man of the Marquis's age could not be delighted by her beauty and feminine charms.

'You may want to be faithful to your Caroline. You may wish to reject my offer, but this is a luxury you cannot afford. My husband has used and enjoyed your Caroline, and he will have his way with her again in future whenever it pleases him. This is something you have no power to prevent and neither do I. You have to take her away from here to a safer place, and this is something I can give you. I will write glowing references for you both and send you to my father's court. I assure you that you'll both be safe there.' She paused. 'But everything has its price, and today you are the price. Do you understand, Philippe? Am I really too terrible a price to pay?'

Philippe closed his eyes and there was a long silence. The Marchioness put down her glass, stood up and walked toward her dressing table. Philippe unbuckled his belt.

A Significant Word

I have never forgotten Marlene Harris. She was someone's sister. During primary school holidays, Les and Frankie fucked her in the old deserted house. She stood on a small pile of bricks and rubble in the cellar and, knickers around her ankles, she lifted her dress. Les and Frankie fucked her and so did the other boys, including her brother. I was younger, but her brother said I could fuck her too if I wanted. It was very generous of him. I don't remember what she said about it, but I think it would have been all right by her too. I don't remember her saying anything to anyone.

I was younger than the others and this was an activity that I had never even imagined before. What a strange thing to do. Why would you want to do that? Would she pee twice as much afterwards?

I don't remember how I managed to express my reticence while still remaining cool. I think I was too young to feel that being cool was important. Maybe the world was still too young to think that being cool was important. It was certainly before my penis had developed any sort of homing instinct. Anyway, it was an opportunity that I passed up without any great sense of loss.

Unfortunately, however, although my penis was not aroused, my curiosity was. I remember that, when I arrived home, my father was sitting at the kitchen table, doing a crossword puzzle. I was standing at the door next to the ice chest when I asked him, 'Daddy, what does "fuck" mean?'

'What!'

I instantly realised that this was not a good question.

Fury flashed in my father's eyes as he sprang to his feet. 'What did you say?'

'I didn't say anything, Daddy. I didn't mean it.'

I raced into the dining room with my father in pursuit. There was nowhere to go really and he caught me in the bedroom as I tried to get under the bed. He grabbed my foot and dragged me out.

'No, Daddy, I didn't say anything. I didn't mean it!' I wasn't sure what I didn't mean, but I was sure I didn't mean it. This had not been a good question to ask.

I tried to dig my heels in as my father dragged me out into the garden. I knew what this meant. He had made a very springy cane from the hedge that surrounded the house. He kept it in the hedge.

'Please no, Daddy. I didn't mean it. I didn't mean it. Please don't, don't hit me!'

I have no recollection of anything my father said to me. I'm not sure why I was so terrified on this occasion. It was just another beating. I suppose it was not so much fear of the thrashing. It was the shock of realisation that this was a very significant word. I had not been aware that words could have such power. In one indelible moment, I realised I should wait until I got back to school to ask about 'cunt'.

The Complete and Utter Truth About the World and Everything In It

I write this brief explanation from my hospital cell before the drugs take effect. The doctors think I am mad. However, the material that follows is an unmodified printout of files that I found at home on one of my computers.

Despite anything the authorities say, I swear that I am absolutely sound of mind, do not have a drinking problem and have not invented the whole thing in the quest for money or notoriety. I have removed periodic outbursts of inarticulate rubbish from the text. These outbursts may be due to the diminishing coherence of this mysterious, extraterrestrial author, but are more likely the typical aberrations of an ageing Atari computer.

*

I know that I am dying. My life systems are closing down. It is better this way. I am an innocent passer-by, a hybrid, a monster, the bastard creation of a life form beyond your comprehension. My father left me long ago. It was not the custom of his planet to raise and protect its young. My mother, an earthling, never knew she had me. I was excreted during what she took to be a brief illness. Maybe she didn't think it was an illness. Maybe chickens don't think.

My life on Earth has not been long compared to my father's and has not been noticed: no more than four or five of your Earth centuries. My father was here from the time of your great lizards. Now he is gone and I am dying.

I have nothing in the way of possessions. They would be of no use, as I have no physical presence on this planet. I leave my farewell message in this gentleman's computer because, despite the silliness of its people, I have become fond of the planet Earth. I leave you this earthly translation of my father's journal, which may, like holding up a mirror, give you some small insight into your own race and the folly which will bring about your extinction if you cannot stop making the same errors.

When I say 'my father's journal', I should perhaps explain that no physical journal actually existed. Once upon a time, when my father's mind was multi-tasking, he must have needed some extra memory or thinking space, so he downloaded a number of files into my memory. In the same way as your young are sometimes inquisitive and go through their parents' drawers, I copied the files and cached them away before my father could reload them and erase them from my memory.

Later on, going through them at leisure, I found that they constituted a journal of my father's time on your planet. As my systems gradually close down, I similarly download these journals on to this man's hard drive. If only I had the energy to reach a better computer! He still has one of those terrible old Ataris. It will probably scramble everything.

*

Jupiday the 79th of Nadjur, in the year 273[17] of the Grand Cycle

What a terrible place! I was starting to wonder about my personal hygiene, but it's all these swamps and methane. So hot and sticky, and all these stupid lizards. What a boring existence! Nothing to do really, except eat each other. It's like a Bungong horror movie. Maybe it's one of those endurance games. I think I might have a nap.

*

Jupiday the 80th of Nadjur, in the year 273[17] GC

That's better! Nothing like a good zizz to clear away the lizards. Maybe it was just a nightmare. Still, today it seems to be monkeys. Whooee! And I thought I needed deodorant!

*

Can't remember what day it is, but it's still Nadjur 273[17] GC

The Cain Mutiny

I know humans think they understand their origins. It's all written in that book *Genesis: the game the whole family can play*. However, the book wasn't written by anyone who was there. None of the people who were there could read or write. I was there. I saw it all. I heard it all.

In the beginning, they say, was the Word, and the Word, so it seems, was with men. Women were blamed for what were called *peccata mundi*, the sins of the world. Eve certainly offered Adam her fruit, but it was always the snake which caused the problems.

In the beginning, Adam and Eve were happy. Of course, until the apple incident, they didn't realise their possibilities. However, Eve was probably as pleased as Adam when they understood how the sum of their parts, the merging of their differences, could create such a warm glow.

In the beginning, there was just one penis in the world. But once their sons, Cain and Abel, became fully aware of their anatomy, they were keen to exploit their capabilities. Adam having a worldwide monopoly on the only human vagina was not an acceptable situation.

In the beginning, they were able to take the matter in hand. Later, word came down that God had pronounced his judgement about spilling one's seed on the ground. It works well for plants, but in the case of humans, the participation of a woman is preferable.

Anyway, how can people accept the story that's handed down? The arithmetic doesn't work. The biology doesn't hang together. I know it's a nice story, except for the unfortunate outcome between Cain and Abel, but human stories are not always nice. Really, a lot of it hangs on the conversation I heard one day between Eve and her adolescent son Cain. He was the elder of the two offspring.

'I love you, Mummy.'

'I love you too, dear.'

'Mummy, how come there aren't any women?'

'There are, dear. I'm a woman.'

'But you're our mummy. Why aren't there any other women?'

'Well, that's the way God made it, dear. There need to be some baby girls and then they can grow up to be women.'

'Right, so how do babies happen? Don't we need some more people? How can we get some more girls?'

'Well, you've seen what Daddy and I do. That's how it happens. That's how you boys happened. I'm sure there will be some girls come along in the fullness of time. I'm not sure that it's right to do that sort of thing with your sister, though, but I'm certain God will give us some guidance on the matter.'

'But Mummy, Daddy doesn't pay much attention to you any more. Does he have to be the one who does it?'

'Yes, dear.'

'Don't you get lonely when he goes hunting?'

'No, dear.'

'Is Daddy still up to it these days? Can't we help?'

'Well, not really, dear. God wouldn't like it.'

'God doesn't have to do it. We could do it for him. Why can't we? We're all family. It's not like we don't know each other.'

'Yes, but this is as close as you and I are supposed to get. To put it bluntly, darling, you're not my meat.'

'Don't you love me, Mummy? If you really loved me, you'd –'

'Forget it, Cain. It's not going to happen.'

'But Mummy, I promise, no kinky stuff. I'll still respect you in the morning, and Daddy doesn't need to know about it.'

'Forget it, Cain.'

'I've been practising with Abel.'

'Your father will beat the living shit out of you if he hears about any of this.'

'No, don't tell Daddy.'

'Maybe Daddy needs to know.'

'No, don't tell Daddy, please… How about just this once?'

'Forget it.'

'We can have a bath first, in the sea even, right away from all the hippo poo and everything.'

'Absolutely not.'

After a silence, 'Can I be first reserve?'

But somehow the Earth's population is now more than seven billion, so it's fairly certain that Eve saw some more action from someone. I was probably having a nap at the time.

*

The Road to Lutetia

I have decided to stop putting the date on my journal entries. The dates are meaningless here on Earth and I am sure some Earthlings will feel a need to calibrate our time against theirs. This is not easily done as earthly time is reasonably linear and ours is measured against the exponential rate at which our star accelerates into the Black Hole of Glonk. The need to measure this kind of thing is, I believe, described by some Earthlings as 'anal'. In our culture we do not have this concept since, having no material or physical manifestation, we have no need for food and, having no need for food, we have no need for an anus.

Even if one has no physical presence in the cosmos, there are times when the weather can be tiresome. Today has been tiresome. Clearly, I use the term 'today' in an earthly context. My existence, in fact, has a clock rate that synchronises and adapts to my immediate universe.

So today I sought refuge from the heat and flies (although I have no anus) and wafted into a small tavern in Lutetia. History reveals that this small town was later to become Paris. A couple was checking in at the front desk and the conversation seemed animated. I tuned in. The concierge was having some difficulty explaining to them that no rooms were available.

'But I'm Mark Antony. I'm a military commander,' insisted one of the hopeful guests.

'How nice for you, sir, and I'm a Vestal Virgin. I'm sorry, sir. I'd ask for your ID, but we're full. There's a cowshed down the street that has some nice double mangers.'

'Look, I'm sure we can come to some sort of arrangement. We've come all the way from Egypt. Can I interest you in some frankincense or myrrh? This is a queen standing beside me.'

'That may be so, sir, but we don't discriminate on the grounds of sexuality.'

'No, I mean a queen, an empress. Can we speak to the manager, please?'

'May I see your ID first, please, sir?'

'What for? I'm a Roman citizen. I'm Marcus Antonius, Mark Antony. Don't you know me, boy? How dare you question me!'

'I'm sorry, sir, but we always need to be on the lookout for illegal immigrants.'

'Is this some kind of discrimination?'

'No, sir, this is the Roman Empire. We'll crucify anyone.' The clerk took their ID documents and went to get the manager.

The man remonstrated with his partner. 'Look, Cleo, I understand you want to get away from it all, but Roman bureaucracy can be a real pain in the arse. You just float above all this stuff in Egypt, but it's not that easy when you get further away from Rome. Anyway, I shouldn't have told them who I am. If Pompey and his lot catch up with us, we'll end up in the river with lead boots.'

'Tony, please. Just a few weeks, then we can go back to Egypt. Shoosh! Here comes the manager.'

The manager was well-groomed and exuded charm.

'Good afternoon, sir. Can I help you?'

'Look, we've come all the way from Egypt and this lady is extremely well-connected. Are you sure you can't organise a room for us?'

'Well, I do have space for madame in my own personal suite, but there's only room for her. I'm afraid *you* will have to move on.'

'Listen, sleazebag, don't get smart with me or I'll have you crucified.'

'I'm afraid you're not in a position to threaten anyone, sir. As you said to the concierge, you're Mark Antony. There's an all-points bulletin out for you. This is Lutetia, you know. We're not a hick town. We've just received last month's news, hot off the mule train. You're a wanted man. I know I'm taking considerable risk here, but I can find space for madame in my very own bed. That's the best I can do. I'm afraid *you*'ll have to move on.'

'Listen, you jumped-up little –'

'Now, now, sir, that will be enough of that!'

'I'll remember this, dogbreath. Just wait till we sort out these other issues. You'll be hanging from a cross. Come on, Cleo. Let's get out of here.'

'Just a moment, Tony. I'm talking to this gentleman. How much are you expecting for a place in your bed?'

'Cleo!'

'Look, madame, I'm a reasonable man. I'm sure we can come to some sort of arrangement.'

'Cleo, what are you talking about? Let's get out of here.'

'Be quiet, Tony. I'm talking to the gentleman. So how big is this bed of yours?'

'Queen-sized, madame'

'What a wonderful coincidence. It just so happens that I'm a queen, and I'm sure that I'm just your size.'

'Cleo!'

'Shut up, Tony!'

'I'm sure we can accommodate madame.'

'And I'm sure I can accommodate you. What did you say your name is, monsieur?'

'Cleo!' insisted her outraged partner.

'Shut up, Tony. Beat it!'

*

Charlemagne and Roland (Charlie goes and Roland blows)

Earthlings have had to put up with such primitive communication systems for a long time. It is difficult for those of us who come from other galaxies to accept that your progression as a life form could be so slow. Your folklore seems to extol examples of such primitive communication.

There is the story of the Holy Roman Emperor Charlemagne and his commander Roland, who had been instructed to sound his elephant horn if he needed reinforcements. In the name of honour, he waited till his dying breath to alert the emperor. How powerful were Roland's lungs? Had he not been dying, deeply punctured by some Saracen sword, he could clearly have been heard from a greater distance. It's like your silly operas, where the heroine is dying of tuberculosis, but holds a high B-flat for eight bars. Anyway, if the limit of your communication is one blast of a trumpet, you cannot allow yourselves to become widely separated. Still, given that radio or the mobile telephone had not then been invented, they had to make do. Nevertheless, it seems that the system was at times problematic.

I was present one day when Charlemagne summoned Roland to his tent.

'Listen, Roland, old boy, I'm afraid I've had a few complaints from the lads.'

'Complaints, Milord? How can anyone complain about serving in your army? There can be no higher honour.'

'Well, actually the complaints aren't about me, old boy. They're about you.'

'Me, Milord? What have I done?'

'Well, it's about all this horn-blowing. The troops feel there's been a bit too much of it.'

'But Milord, a man needs to practise. How can I summon reinforcements to rescue us if I don't keep my chops up?'

'Yes, I know you need to practise, but yesterday morning you had a blow and two hundred and thirty men came racing back from the latrines. At least we'll know the way to the latrines in future. They left a trail.'

'Milord, surely this shows our procedures are sound.'

'Perhaps, but I must confess I have my own concerns. What's this business with the trombone? I like the horn. Why have you been practising trombone?'

'Milord, I just thought we could do with some other fellows capable of filling the role, in case I run out of puff. And I thought we need a bit of variety. A little bit of trumpet goes a long way.'

'Exactly. That's the point, Roland. People can hear you from miles away.'

'Of course I'll still play lead horn, Milord, but I think we could back it up with some other instrumentation. I was thinking of a small jazz band.'

'Look, Roland, we know diversity is commendable, but no self-respecting soldier will be seen playing flute or clarinet.'

'How about cor anglais? We can scare the hell out of the enemy.'

'Roland, you've got to be joking. You'll scare our own men.'

'Guitar, Milord? If we invest in some generators, we can have electric guitar. That will keep the enemy at a distance.'

'Well, I know you'll pull more chicks if you play guitar, but…'

*

Thomas Beckett

And then there was that archbishop fellow, Thomas Becket. He came to a very messy end. Most unpleasant business. The soldiers didn't say much. Quite inarticulate really. All action and no talk. Is that what you Earthlings say? The archbishop seemed to do all the talking. He was not very pleased.

'Excuse me, gentlemen. This is a cathedral. You can't do that here. Could you leave your horses outside, please. I say, excuse me…excuse me. Look, do you have any plastic bags with you? Just look what your horses have done. There's dung all the way up the aisle. When you've put your horses outside, could you please come back and clean up some of this mess? People kneel on these floors. People prostrate themselves. I shan't hear confession from you while there's any of that left on the floor. If you don't behave in a respectful fashion, I shall report this to the king. I happen to have a very close relationship with the king. Er, sorry gentlemen, helmets off in the house of God, no weapons in here, please. Put the sword down, please, sir. Put the sword down, I say. Please put –'

It seems the soldiers involved in this unfriendly situation believed they were acting at the behest of their king, Henry II of England. Thomas Becket, the Archbishop of Canterbury, was opposing Henry's will and Henry had wished someone would rid him of this nuisance. At the time, the grievance was probably exacerbated by Henry's difficult relationship with his official wife, Eleanor of Aquitaine, who also had a very prickly personality. Not long after Becket's murder in the cathedral, I overheard a colourful discussion between the King and his Queen.

*

Eleanor of Aquitaine & Henry II

'No, Henry, I will not give you a divorce. I heard what they did to Thomas Becket. You really are a churlish rogue, Henry. You brook absolutely no opposition from anyone who comes between your sad little penis and its current interest.'

'You criticise me! At least I didn't get off with my Uncle Raymond.'

'Maybe he was a better lover than your father. And at least Raymond was only a couple of years older than me, not an old man like your father and not a boy like you.'

'Well, I'm not sure about the ins and outs of all that, but give me credit for not taking my father's advice. He said you had a vagina like a horse collar.'

'Don't be coarse, you sad, little whoremonger. Unlike you, I haven't run around bedding everything that moves. Maybe you'd profit from the treatment they handed out to that Pierre Abelard.'

'I don't think so. I'm still putting my bollocks to good use.'

'You're wasting them on that cheap Rosamund woman.'

'Well, at least I don't poonce around in Poitiers conducting some effeminate "court of love" with half-mast, halfwit, half-arsed poets who would rather make love to their hand than a woman.'

'You are such a buffoon, Henry. Just because you control England, Normandy, Brittany, Anjou and Aquitaine. Your only attraction lies in your power and your property, and you struggle on with some vain idea that your charm lies within your pants.'

'Well, I have given you eight children.'

'That's what you think. And even if some of them are yours, they're still mongrels, most of them.'

'I can't help but believe they are bastards, plotting with their mother against their father and their king.'

'Rubbish, Henry. Just because they raised an army against you. Release me.'

'No, my dear, I simply can't trust you. I'm afraid you must remain in detention indefinitely.'

And so it appears that even if humans are of noble birth, they still seem to have the same kind of relationships within their marriages.

*

Joan of Arc: The principles of parenting

Life here on Earth is so primitive. However, in my time here, I have had the opportunity to observe some more commendable qualities amongst the foolishness. I said previously it was not the custom of my father's planet to raise and protect its young. Parents here are very protective until their offspring have outgrown the folly of their youth.

I am reminded of an occasion in France during what Earthlings would call the fifteenth century. I was aware of the very electric atmosphere emanating from a small, modest cottage and, not being restricted by any physical dimensions, I let myself in.

The father was extremely agitated. 'What do you mean, you want to go to Chinon. That's halfway across France. What's in Chinon?'

'The king is in Chinon,' the daughter replied.

'So what? What's that to you? What's that to us?'

'God wants me to go.'

'God wants you to go! Lord preserve us! What kind of blasphemy is this?'

'I have a message for the king,' Joan announced.

'You have a message for the king! Have you taken leave of your senses?'

'No, Father.'

'And how, pray tell, do you think you are going to get to Chinon? It's halfway across France. Have you any idea how dangerous it would be? How do you think you can get to Chinon in safety?'

'Fear not, Father. In my dream, I go with soldiers.'

At this point the mother interrupted. 'With soldiers? What do you mean, with soldiers? Lord have mercy! You think you'll be safe with soldiers? And who will protect you from the soldiers?'

'God will protect me, Mother, and I will protect the soldiers.'

'Sweet Jesus, my daughter has lost her mind. And are you going to walk or will you sit on the knee of a soldier?'

'I will ride a horse, Mother.'

'We don't have a horse, you wretched girl. Are the soldiers going to give you a horse? Is this the price they will pay to ride my daughter? You don't know how to ride a horse. And if they find a horse for you, where will you find a side-saddle?'

'I won't ride side-saddle, Mother. I will use a man's saddle.'

Father returned to the fray, 'What do you mean, a man's saddle? You will ride with a horse between your legs? Rubbing against your womanhood? Against your girlhood? This is disgraceful. And what do you think people will say? They will say you find pleasure in this. And what about your maidenhead? You will destroy your maidenhead. No man will want you. We will be blamed.'

'Father, my maidenhead is gone. I don't know if I ever had a maidenhead. It isn't there.'

'What do you mean, it's not there? How do you know?'

'It is not there, Father. I know. I can feel it is not there.'

The father gave her a resounding slap across the face. 'You know this with your own fingers? You dirty little girl! What will the neighbours say?'

'The neighbours will not know, Father.'

He hit her again on the same cheek, which was already bright red, as the blood rushed to her face.

Mother returned to the discussion. 'Disgraceful child to touch yourself. I hope you realise God saw you do that.'

'Of course he did. God sees everything. He knows everything I do. He knows my body better than I do. He sees me naked every day.'

This time it was the mother who hit her. 'You impudent girl, what interest would he have in a child like you?'

'He loves us all, Mother. I know he likes my body. The mirror and the windows become misty when he sees me.'

The father gave her a resounding slap on the arm. 'Blasphemous child! What will people think? And this fanciful journey to Chinon, where do you think you will sleep? With the soldiers?'

'The journey will be dangerous. I will sleep with the soldiers and protect them.'

In more 'modern' times, I have heard parents confronted with this situation ask their offspring if they have packed a change of underwear, socks, pyjamas. Have they packed some sandwiches and fruit for the trip? It is interesting to see how much culture can change with the passage of time. I have heard 'modern' boys and girls discuss the effectiveness of using Gladwrap if the need arises. I remain slightly puzzled about this. However, there is probably a considerable range of plastic wrapping for people's sandwiches.

*

Tom and Harry (Henry VIII and More)

And then there was that king, the one with all the wives. I was surprised to overhear his discussion with Sir Thomas More, another churchman. There were plays and films that portrayed the discussion quite poetically but, as I heard it, the actual conversation was a lot more to the point.

'Listen, Thomas, it's a matter of religious principle, and besides, I want to put my penis in her vagina and squirt.'

'His Majesty describes the issue quite articulately. Firstly, however, it is common knowledge that His Majesty has not bothered to wait for His Holiness's ruling on the matter. Secondly, I fear his understanding of religious principles may be coloured by his enthusiasm for this lady.'

'Look, Thomas, I'm sure we can discuss this reasonably, or I'll have you beheaded. Don't talk to me about principles. I'm king and you're just a churchman. What the fuck did Christ know about Christianity? I'm a king. No, not just a king, I'm *the* King.'

'With all due respect, Your Majesty, the Holy Bible is quite explicit in relation to these issues of earthly passion.'

'Thomas, you know nothing about this. Her vagina wins out every time against your Bible. You know nothing about her vagina. If you do, I'll have you executed.'

'In this matter, I must concede, His Highness's expertise is unsurpassed. However, in terms of spiritual guidance, I feel obliged to remind His Majesty of the risk to his mortal soul and its place in eternity.'

'Look, Thomas, you really are being a right prat.'

During this period of earthly history, kings were clearly not people with whom one could disagree. It seems people's heads were removed with an axe. Our custom of vaporisation is considerably less messy. No one has to clean up afterwards. I am confident humans could profit greatly if they learnt from our culture. This whole discussion would have been calmer and much less dangerous if Henry had merely wished to inseminate a chicken.

*

Captain Cook and The Land Down Under

I was briefly present when some of the Europeans first went to that strange southern island they called Terra Nullarbor (or something similar). They've renamed it Australia now. They weren't really the first to go there but, as everywhere in the universe, the victors always get to rewrite history to suit themselves. Their leader, Captain James Cook, seemed to have an amicable relationship with the ship's botanist, Joseph Banks. I still remember a discussion they had one morning.

'Banks, old chap, do come in. Have a seat.'

'Thank you, Captain.'

'Can I offer you a glass of this excellent Spanish sherry?'

'Why not, sir? After all, we've had breakfast.'

'Precisely. Afraid I only have the one sherry glass. The others were broken in that last storm.'

'All's well, Captain. Any port in a storm.'

'Very witty, Banks, but we're drinking sherry, not port. Tell you what, you take the stemmed glass. I'll use this beer tankard.'

'Whatever you say, Captain.'

'Of course. I'm the Captain. So how are the drawings going? Have you discovered any new plants?'

'Captain, almost all the plants here are completely different. I suppose they need to be in order to survive this wretched climate.'

'So do the people. You need to draw some of the native girls. There are some very interesting specimens.'

'Yes, sir, but I think my wife would prefer I limit my interests to the botanical life.'

'Yes, of course. I have my own wife back in England and I do miss her, but a man needs to do what a man needs to do. I tell you, old chap, for a younger man, this country is an excellent deal. We get the country and we get their women on the side. For God's sake, don't tell my wife I said that.'

'No, sir.'

'We just need to close the deal here fairly quickly and move on. There are some great possibilities out there in the Pacific Islands. Not so much land, but lots of women. A bit of a concern the other day, though. I saw one of our crew holding his old boy and, I tell you, it looked like he was squeezing a tube of toothpaste. Blasted pox. He says he had it before he left Europe, but I'm sure it's not going to help tourism if it catches on.'

'No, sir, but we can blame the natives when we get back home.'

'My dear Banks, and how do you intend to tell people we caught it from them? Caught it from the toilet seat?'

'Ah indeed, sir. Perhaps not.'

'Jolly fine sherry, what? Care for another glass?'

'Well, sir, I suppose it is after breakfast.'

*

At this point I am beginning MVG:X>+CY.7FY^CIZO'R_3U]O?X ^?H1``(!` @0$`P0'!00$$``$``$$``$$`P'!`@ to have difficulty saving files. I think MV8)(;'75M$Q:N:]AYEYE00$';:: this miserable little Atari computer is #?KQ2 8?]8OY?2IZC5S&5*%fmG&%$ starting to corrupt 1CB->P]*S90\.>>!_1CB->P]*S90\.>>!_ just when I wanted to tell you about this splendid little fellow, Hitler.

M!4A,08205$'87$3(C*!'!1'D:&QP0DC,U+P%6)RT0H6)#3A)?$7&!D:)B<HM*2HU-C<X.3I#1$5&1TA)2E-455976%E:81E9F=H:6IS='5V=WAY>H*#A(WF5F5(6&<Q3D1$5&1Q5VM[BYNL+#Q,7JXC\C)RM+3U-76MUC9VN+CY.7FY^CIZO+S]/7V]_CY^O_`!$$(`8(`^@,!$$``$$``$$```#(*A?$]M0$(``^@,!$$``$$```$$``RJHQ85V]`_Q9(2^28[>!!CB->P]*S90\.>>!_WR*2 &8XZ+_P!\B@!N\C^ also about the future of the Planet Earth and M&'- #?KQ2 8?]8OY?2IZC5S so I think I can safely tell you that MU]C9VN+CY.7FY^CIZO+S]/7V]_CY^O_ `!$$(`8(`^@,!$$``$$``$$``$$``D.??_&?L?i8W[:)XBL?[.UB(9S@>7 glerk schloompf boidl toonk…

www.ingramcontent.com/pod-product-compliance
Lightning Source LLC
Chambersburg PA
CBHW020348110726
47898CB00003B/1085